for David

First published in paperback in Great Britain by HarperCollins Children's Books in 2008

1 3 5 7 9 10 8 6 4 2

ISBN-13: 978-0-00-726288-5
ISBN-10: 0-00-726288-4

HarperCollins Children's Books is a division of HarperCollins Publishers Ltd.

Text and illustrations copyright © Yokococo 2008

Printed in China

LiTTLE GHOST WICKY

by

Yokococo

HarperCollins *Children's Books*

far away,
on top of a hill,
there was a spooky old house.
A Haunted House!

In the haunted house,
lived a little ghost called Wicky.
His grandad lived in the clock.

Wicky wasn't allowed out of the house.
"It's dangerous outside," said Grandad.
"Ghosts disappear outside."

But Wicky loved to peep
through the curtains
when the sun was shining.

"No, Wicky!" said Grandad.

And Wicky loved to peep
through the window
when the stars were out.

"No, Wicky!" said Grandad.

Day after day,
Wicky looked out of
the window. Then one
rainy afternoon, he suddenly
saw bubbles coming up from
the pond. As each bubble popped,
he heard a voice, giggling...

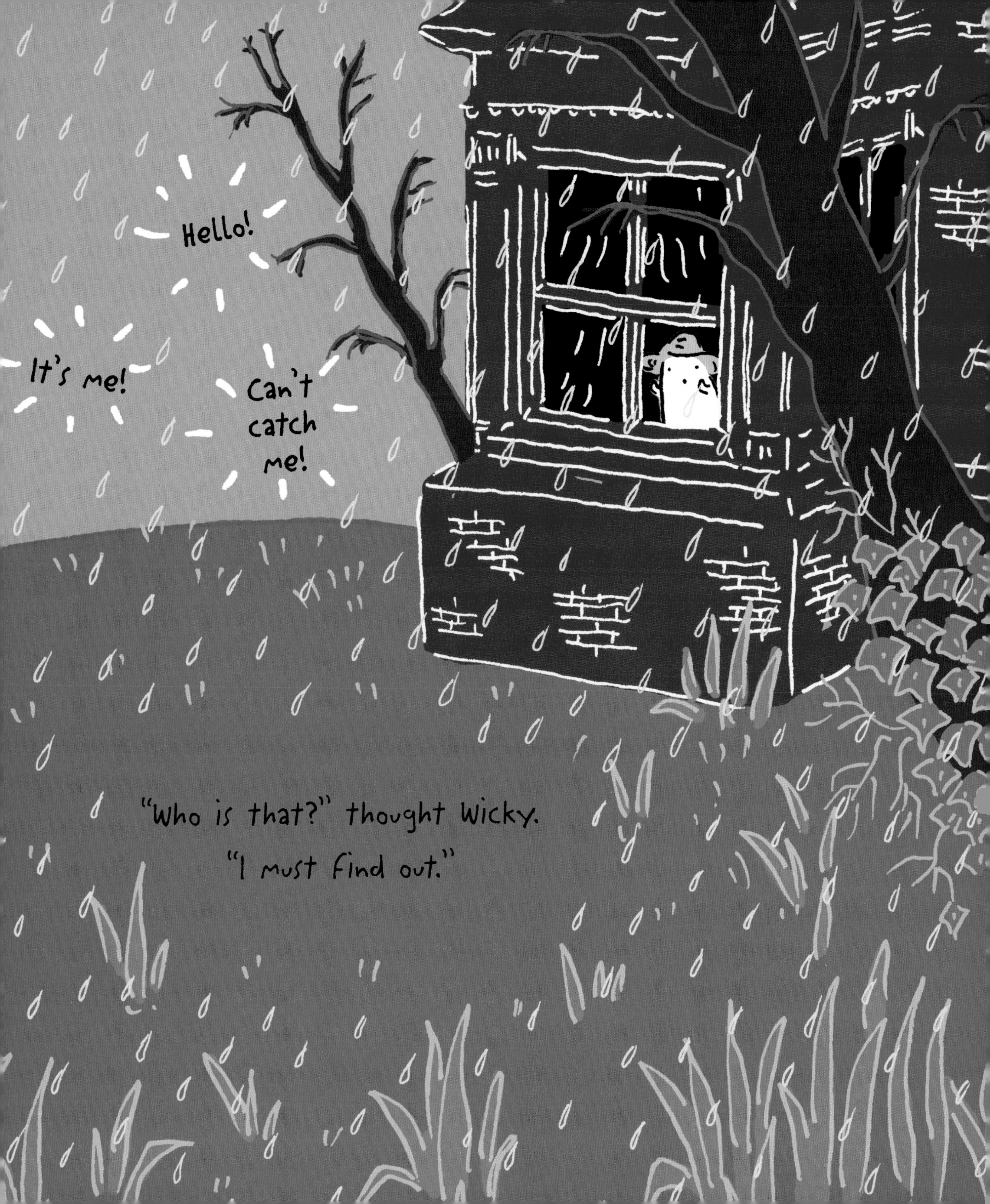

"Who is that?" thought Wicky.
"I must find out."

First Wicky tried to creep out when he thought Grandad wasn't looking.

"Come back, Wicky!" said Grandad.

Next he tried to
creep out in disguise.

"I know it's you, Wicky!" said Grandad.

Then Wicky had a really good idea...

He blew up a balloon,

put a sheet over it,

drew a face and gave
it a hat.

Now Grandad
would think Wicky
was very well-behave

Finally, Wicky squeezed through a gap in the window. At last, he was free!

Wicky looked around. The air was sweet, the moon was bright and, no, he hadn't disappeared. Grandad was wrong!

He looked in the water
and saw... a ghost!

"Can't catch me!"
said the ghost, and was gone.

"Come back!"
cried Wicky.

"I'm Sweetie,"
laughed the little ghost.

He dived down
and down
and down.

"I'm Wicky," said Wicky.
"Wait for me!"

"Can't catch me!" said Sweetie,
and wherever she went in the garden,
flowers sprang up like magic.
Wicky chased after her. It was such fun!

Back inside the house, Grandad was talking to the balloon. "Wicky, you are very well-behaved today!" There was no answer.

"Wicky?" said Grandad. No answer.

There was something
wrong. Grandad had
to take a closer look.

It wasn't Wicky at all!

"Wicky, where are you?"
called Grandad.
And he looked all over
the house but Wicky
was nowhere to be found.

Suddenly, he heard laughter
outside. And there was Wicky,
playing... with another ghost!

Without a moment
to lose, Grandad
whooshed outside.

"Wicky!" said Grandad.
"Grandad!" said Wicky.

"Wicky! Come back indoors now!
We'll all disappear forever!"

But it was too late. The sun was rising...
they were beginning to fade away!

"I'm see through!" cried Wicky.
And so was Grandad. And Sweetie.

"Don't worry," she laughed.
"We're invisible in the sunshine, but we're still here."

"It's true! We haven't disappeared!"
Wicky shouted for joy.

From then on,
nothing was ever the same again.
Grandad still wasn't quite sure
about the open air, but every day
Wicky and Sweetie played
in the sunshine...

...and every night
they danced beneath
the stars.